USBORNE FIRST READING
Level Four

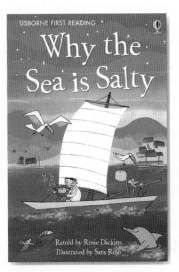

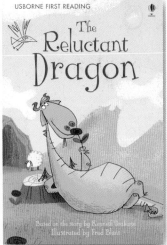

Cinderella

Retold by Susanna Davidson

Illustrated by Lorena Alvarez

Reading consultant: Alison Kelly
University of Roehampton

Once upon a time, there was an unhappy girl named Cinderella.

She was always
dusty and dirty.

All day, she had to cook for her stepmother and clean up after her stepsisters.

At night, she slept on the
floor by the fire.

Her stepsisters were bossy.

Her stepmother was cruel.

But Cinderella was always
loving and kind.

One day, an invitation
arrived.

To all the ladies of the house -
the King invites you to
A Royal Ball
for his son,
Prince Charming.

"Of course Cinderella can't go," said her stepmother. "*She's* just a servant."

Cinderella made her stepsisters' dresses.

She painted their faces and
curled their hair.

11

She watched them step into
the carriage and drive away.

Then Cinderella sat down
by the fire and wept.

"What is it?" asked a gentle voice. "What's the matter?"

"Oh!" cried Cinderella.

A fairy stood before her, in a swirl of stars.

I'm your fairy godmother.

"Why are you crying?" the fairy asked.

"I want to go to the ball," sobbed Cinderella.

"And so you shall," said the fairy. "But first, we'll need a pumpkin."

Cinderella ran into
the garden and picked
the biggest pumpkin
she could find.

"Stand back!" said the
fairy. She tapped the
pumpkin with her wand.

Abracadabra!

Sparkles shot through the air. The pumpkin rose up, growing bigger and rounder. Then BANG!

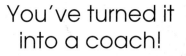

You've turned it into a coach!

"Now, I need a mousetrap,"
the fairy went on.

Six mice ran out. The fairy
tapped each one.

They turned into six proud horses, tossing their silky manes.

"What shall we do for a coachman?" asked the fairy.

The rat in the trap
looked hopeful.

Yes,
you'll do!

"For my next spell, I need six lizards!"

"Here!" called Cinderella. "Behind the watering can."

With a wave of the wand they were footmen, dressed in glittering green.

Cinderella looked down at
her tattered clothes.
The fairy raised her wand
one last time.

Cinderella's rags vanished.
She wore a golden ballgown,
laced with flowers.

On her feet were glass
slippers – the prettiest she'd
ever seen.

"Just remember! You must leave before the clock strikes midnight."

Then my magic will start to fade.

Cinderella waved from the carriage.

The horses galloped away.

She walked into the palace
and gazed around in wonder.

29

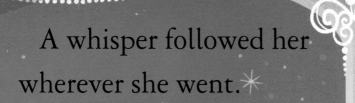

A whisper followed her
wherever she went.

Who is that beautiful girl?

The Prince saw Cinderella.
He rushed up to her.

Cinderella put her hand in his. They glided across the ballroom.

Cinderella's stepsisters
watched. They thought she
must be a princess.

I bet the Prince would rather dance with me.

Cinderella and the Prince
danced and danced, until
the clock struck midnight.

Cinderella dashed away.
As she ran down the palace
steps...

...her dress turned back
to rags.

Her carriage was a pumpkin.
Her coachman was a rat.

Cinderella ran home on
bare feet, beneath the
starry sky.

The Prince hurried after her.

All that was left was a glass slipper, sparkling on the steps.

At home, Cinderella waited for her stepsisters.

"How was the ball?"
she asked.

"A princess came," they said.

"The Prince danced with her *all* night. Otherwise he would have danced with us."

"She ran away at the end. I wonder if he'll ever find her?"

39

Cinderella smiled a secret smile, but said nothing.

Two days' later, the King's trumpet sounded in the street.

The Prince went from house to house. Every girl wanted to try on the shoe.

At last, they came to Cinderella's house.

Her stepsisters tried to squeeze into the shoe.

Cinderella came quietly into the room.

"May I try it on?" she asked.

It was a perfect fit.

Cinderella pulled the other glass slipper from her pocket.

As she put it on, the room lit up with stars. Her rags turned back into a ballgown.

"At last!" cried the Prince. "I've found you. Will you marry me?"

"Yes!" replied Cinderella.

Everyone was invited to the
wedding – even the stepsisters.

Cinderella had such a kind heart, she forgave her family...

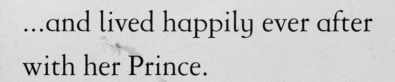

...and lived happily ever after with her Prince.

About the story

Cinderella is an old, old story. It was first told in Ancient Egypt and today there are over 700 different versions. This one is from a retelling by Charles Perrault, called *Cinderella, or The Little Glass Slipper*.

Designed by Caroline Spatz
Series designer: Russell Punter
Series editor: Lesley Sims

First published in 2013 by Usborne Publishing Ltd., Usborne House, 83-85 Saffron Hill, London EC1N 8RT, England. www.usborne.com
Copyright © 2013 Usborne Publishing Ltd.

48

USBORNE FIRST READING
Level Four

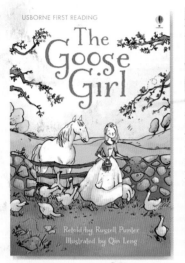

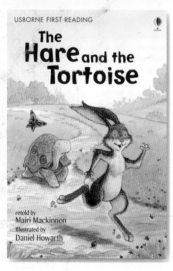

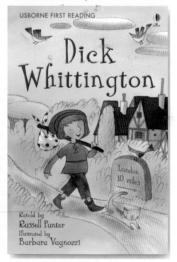